A Golden Book®

Golden Books Publishing Company, Inc.,
Racine, Wisconsin 53404, USA

Golden Books & Design™ , A Golden Book® and related
trademarks and service marks are the property of
Golden Books Publishing Company, Inc.

Published in 1997 in the U.K. by
Golden Books Publishing Company, Inc.,
25-31 Tavistock Place, London WC1H 9SU

Created and produced by
Magi Publications, London

Text © 1997 by Martin Hall
Illustrations © 1997 by Joanne Moss

Printed in Italy

ISBN 0 307 81504 8

Looking For Puppy

by Martin Hall

illustrated by Joanne Moss

GOLDEN BOOKS™

Sarah and her teddy, Bran, were looking for Puppy.

'Puppy! Puppy! Puppy!' called Sarah. He was so new that he didn't have a name yet. They looked all over the house for him.

First, Sarah pushed Bran underneath the beds to see if Puppy was hiding there, but he wasn't.

Together Sarah and Bran searched
all the cupboards and wardrobes,
but they couldn't find Puppy
anywhere.
Next they looked in the bathroom.
Sarah even fetched a stool and
peeped over the top of the
tall laundry basket.

The cupboard under the stairs was a bit scary, but Sarah and Bran looked there, too.
Sarah was very careful, because she thought that there might be spiders lurking . . .
'Don't worry, Bran, we'll find Puppy,' said Sarah. She was trying not to cry.

Perhaps Puppy was in the garden?
'He will be so cold and frightened
out there,' said Sarah.
She knew Mum and Dad would be
cross if she went into the garden
alone when it was dark and snowy,
but she had to find Puppy.
'We must be very quiet,' she
whispered to Bran. She put on
a warm coat and tied a scarf round
Bran's neck . . .

. . . and out crept Sarah and Bran.
The garden was not the same
friendly place that it was in the
daytime. It felt really spooky.
The light from the kitchen
window didn't reach far and the
shadows lapped at its edges.
'Puppy! Puppy!' cried Sarah.
Something rustled, but it was only
the wind in the bare branches of
the trees.

Someone was standing in the
middle of the lawn. It was
a man, wearing a hat.
Sarah's heart went
thump-thump.
Who was it?

Just then, the moon came out from
behind a cloud and bathed the
garden in cold light. Sarah saw that
the man was only the snowman she
had made the day before. Then she
noticed some little pawmarks
leading towards the shed.

'Come on, Bran,' said Sarah.
'Let's see if Puppy's there.
He must be very frightened.'
She was a bit frightened herself.
They crept down the garden,
opened the shed door . . .

. . . and a big white shape flew
off the roof.
'SCREECH! SCREECH!'
it went. Sarah screamed.
She didn't stop to look in the
shed. She ran back to the house
as fast as she could . . .

. . . and right into Mum's arms.
'You naughty girl!' said Mum.
'What were you doing, out there
all alone?'
'Looking for Puppy,' said Sarah.
'But a spooky ghost frightened me.'

They went back to the warm
kitchen, where Dad had laid the
table for supper.
Suddenly Sarah remembered
something.
'Where's Bran? Oh Mum,
I've lost Bran
as well as
Puppy!'

'You must have dropped him in the garden,' said Dad. 'I'll go out and look for them both.'
Just as Dad was pulling on his coat, there was a noise at the door —
an excited, scrabbling sort of noise.
Mum went to open it . . .

. . . and in ran Puppy, with Bran
dangling from his mouth.
'Look!' said Dad. 'Puppy must
have been shut in the shed!'
'Puppy's found Bran, and Bran's
found Puppy!' cried Sarah,
hugging them both.

'And I know just the name for
Puppy,' said Mum. *'Spooky!'*